CAN YOU H
ME, GRANDAD?

by

Pat Thomson

Illustrated by

Jez Alborough

VICTOR GOLLANCZ LTD
LONDON 1986

Hello, Grandad.
We are going to have a treat.
We're going to the zoo.

What's that? Glue?
You've fallen in the glue?
Never mind. Just don't sit down
and you'll be all right.

Not glue, Grandad, zoo.
We're going to the zoo.
I expect we'll go on the train.

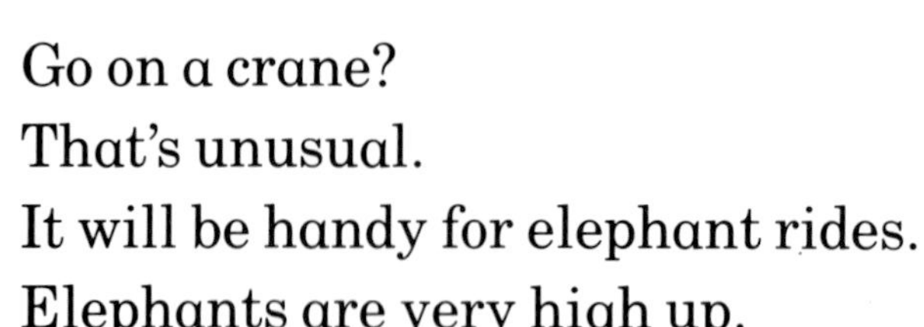

Go on a crane?
That's unusual.
It will be handy for elephant rides.
Elephants are very high up.

Not crane, Grandad, train.
Are you a bit deaf today,
or are you teasing?
Mum says I must sit beside her.

Sit on a tiger? Your Mum?
Isn't she amazing!
What a brave woman.

Not a tiger, Grandad, beside her.
I must sit beside her on the train.
We're going to take our tea.

Going to see the flea?
Do they have fleas in zoos these days?
You can borrow my glasses, if you like.

Not flea, Grandad, tea.
Mum wants to see the leopards.
She told me there's a saying,
'A leopard cannot change its spots'.

Cannot change its socks?
Phew! That's terrible.
It must be dreadful in hot weather.

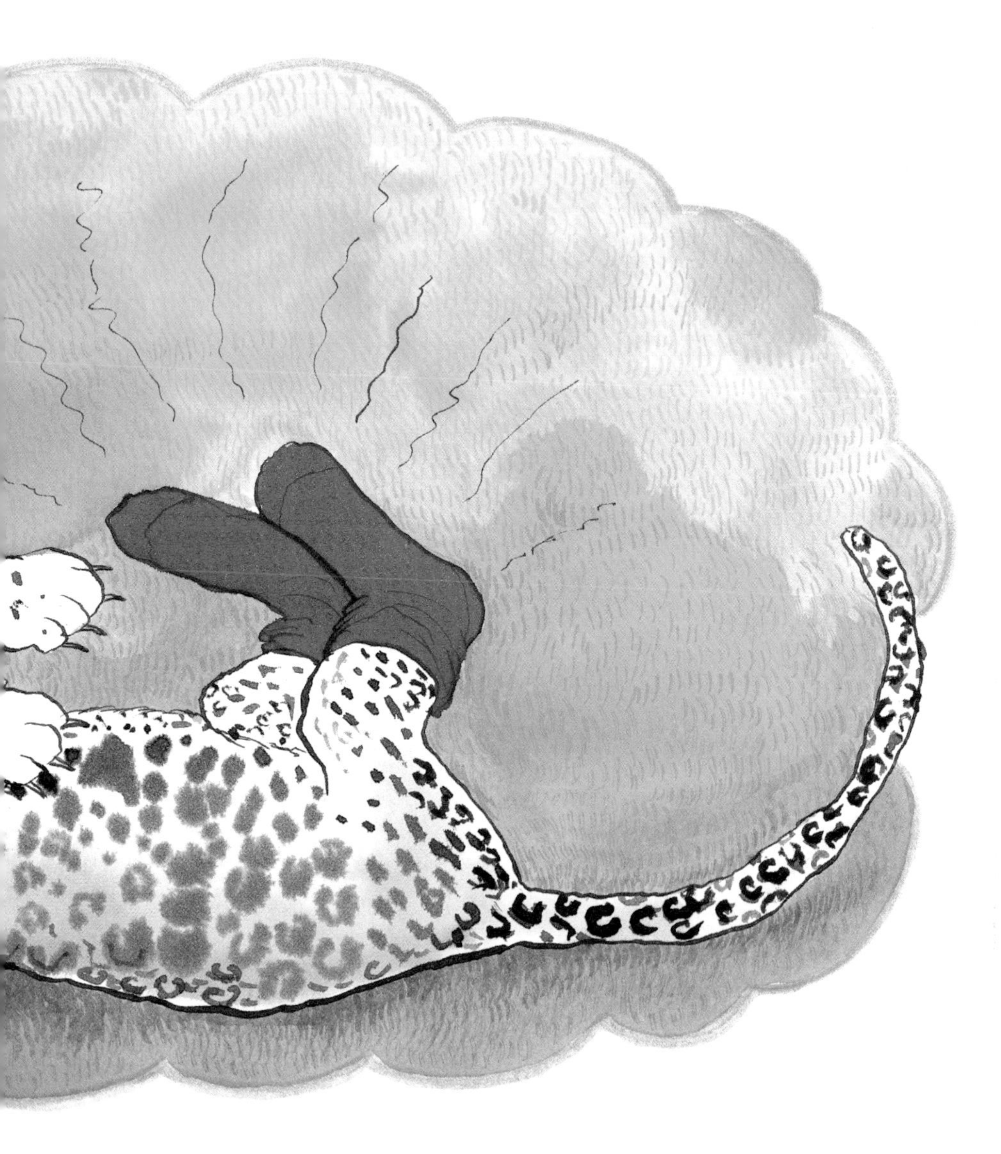

Not socks, Grandad, spots.
You are trying to make me laugh.
Did you know that lions and leopards
are called the big cats?

Wear big hats, do they?
It's to keep the sun off, no doubt.
They come from very hot countries.

Not big hats, Grandad, big cats.
They belong to the cat family.
I learned that at school.

Leaned over the pool?
The sea lion pool?
If you fall in,
I'll come and feed you with fish.

Not pool, Grandad, school.
I won't fall in.
I don't want a fish moustache
like the sea lions.
I shall go for a ride.
You can even ride on the llamas.

Go in your pyjamas?
Whatever next!
I hope there are no
holes in them.

Not pyjamas, Grandad, llamas.
I'm not going to show
everyone my pyjamas.
I'll go and see the parrots,
I'd like to see them flying about.

Carrots flying about?
You must keep your head down.
You don't want to be knocked out
by a carrot.

Not carrots, Grandad, parrots.
Do you think we'll see
the giant anteater?

Giant aunt-eater?
Must be big.
I doubt if it would manage
your Auntie Mabel.

Not aunt-eater, Grandad, anteater.
I'll go and see the bears, too.
They live in a cave.

Give them a shave?
Why do you want to do that?
Bears don't know where their
coats end and their beards begin.

Cave, Grandad, not shave.
You are a terrible tease today.
Well, I like all the animals
but I think I like the monkeys best.

You'd like to be the monkeys' guest?
Yes, you would like that.
Up there in the trees,
monkeying around.
I expect you will enjoy your visit.

Mum asked if you would like
to come too.
Would you like to come
to the zoo with us?

My goodness, how clearly you speak
for someone so young.
Yes, I'd love to come.
I want to see the reindeer,
so I'd better fetch my umbrella.